D1714343

Warning:

This short story is not for the faint of heart or sensitive minds. Aggressive and highly sexual, beastly content is expressed within. A quick and exceedingly ravaging centaur and human woman gangbang. Do not read if you will be offended by this work, or under the age of eighteen. The author or publisher will not be responsible for any offense taken by the reader. This warning should be read and understood before reading or purchasing this book.

Do not read if you cannot handle or accept graphic content and vivid wording.

Erotic Encounters

of the Centaurs

ISBN-13: 978-1492792031

ISBN-10: 1492792039

Chapter 1- Their Virgin Sub

Ginny ran through the forest as fast as her ill-toned legs could carry her. Being raised and pampered in the palace did not prepare her for the exertions she experienced today. The Rain Palace had been her home and free of war since before she was born, so it had come as a surprise when warriors swarmed the palace, helping themselves to all the virgin princesses like a banquet. During the invasion, among screaming girls, her family, Ginny had barely escaped the hardened men, and fled through the forest. Never having seen a man before, from her isolated existence, she had been dumbstruck until witnessing the savagery of them slaking their lusts on her sisters. Fear and a great flight instinct had spurred her feet to move, even now, knowing no one followed, she couldn't slow. Her heart pumped wildly in her chest, her legs having a mind of their own, and beads of sweat rolling down her back instantly had chilled her.

It was so dark only night pods; tulip-like flowers, glowed brightly guiding her flight. Running barefoot among leaves and soft moss protected her pedicured feet. Only a light swath of thin fabric swishing in the wind and clinging to her legs covered her moonlit body. It wasn't much, but that had never crossed her mind, considering the naturally heated pools inside the palace kept her warm year after year.

Gnarly roots growing out of the ground tripped her causing her to land with a heavy thud, nearly knocking the wind from her. She groaned and dug her fingers into the damp earth to regain her footing. Lifting her chest from the forest floor, she looked wildly around, the immediate feeling of exhaustion slammed through her body, rendering her legs useless. She clawed her way under a fallen tree that rested against large boulders, dragging her twitching legs along. It wasn't an ideal hiding spot, but it made her feel a small sense of security. She bit her fist and stifled a whimper when she heard voices.

"Are you sure they were planning a raid at the Rain Palace?" A masculine voice sounded befuddled.

"Aye, I heard it myself. What a mess." A second voice answered regretfully.

"Those poor girls; from what I hear the Rain Palace had been a peaceful haven for many years. The females that live there, never see males and are more secluded than those," The third man snapped his fingers as he thought for the word he needed. "Abbys, ya 'know the place where the women all marry their one God and live there their whole lives?"

The second voice spoke up again. "Those poor females."

"Those poor females? Have you forgotten the treaty broken to us by the Rain Palace those many years ago? The reason the Rain Palace ever existed was because of us. It was our labor and the magic of our ancestors-wasted for that place." The first speaker grumbled.

Ginny had kept shockingly silent, which shouldn't have been hard to do on a normal day, considering there were times the girls all took short vows of silence; but, with her fear nearly choking her, she never thought it would be possible to achieve. She peeked her eye open only to see hooves, horse's hooves. She had seen plenty of the wild beasts from the tower room windows at the palace. Never leaving the sanctuary of her peaceful home, she had never gotten a close look. The closest of the trio of beasts was moving closer, apparently leaning his flanks along the log. Ginny felt the weight of the log pushing her farther into the ground and she fought back her panic.

"So who was the head of the raid?" One of the voices asked, to her discovery, it was the beast leaning against the log. Oh why can't he move his horse away? She silently asked.

"The Arru'Feltons I believe."

"Those imbeciles? Ha-and here I thought it would be a stronger force like Errah'Havvarh."

"Arru'Feltons or Errah'Havvarh, it matters not to any of us. When the humans ran us out, it became our problem no longer. Phen; Darr, let's get out of here and head back home. There is obviously no game for us to hunt and I would rather head to the shack for the rest of the night."

"Ha-ha! Yeah! I hear there is a pretty little filly who brushes the males down with her bare hands."

"Oh shut it, Phen. Your attitude is what scares the new mares off. Do you really want that bumbling idiot Alex giving you a rub down?"

"A'right, a'right; let's go!"

The horse leaning against the log Ginny was under moved some more and a groan slipped from her lips before she could call it back.

"Did you hear that?" One of them asked.

"There may be something to hunt after all. What do you think? Could have been a bear?"

"No, it sounded close and small; maybe something smaller. A boar?" One of them spoke softly.

Ginny hadn't realized her hand was resting farther out from under the log, until a large horse hoof stepped on her fingers. She let out a scream, never feeling such a painful sensation before.

"Gods of equine! What was that?"

"Darr lift your hoof. Something is under that log and I believe you caught it."

The weight from the log lifted thankfully and Ginny gulped in deep breaths, and couldn't miss the smell of moss and damp earth. Tears burned her eyes as a hand wrapped around her wrist to haul her out. She cried out in surprise and the brief twinge of pain that shot up her arm.

"Well I'll be it's a human."

"That's not just a human, that's a female human. What do you think Erric?"

"Judging by her robes, she's from the Rain Palace. Look at the jeweled anklet; it has the rubies from our ruins along it."

"Are you from the Rain Palace, female?"

Ginny looked up, her mouth dropped open; she wasn't looking at horses with riders. She was looking at a beast with a horse body and human torso and upper body. Whatever these monstrosities were; they were very large.

"Do you think she is daft?" One male whispered to another.

"Naw-she's just scared. I don't think they teach their girls about centaurs anymore." The dark man leaned down to look into her eyes.

"Is that it? Are you uneducated about us?"

"I…I haven't h…h-heard about you before." Ginny stammered.

The blond male leaned down to grip her upper arm and hauled her to her feet.

"I am Phen; what is your name little one?"

"Ginny." She said with wide eyes and a dry tongue.

"Well that funny looking guy with the dark hair is Darr." He gestured to his right, and then turned her so her back was against him.

"And the other dark fellow is Erric. Are there any more like you running around?"

"No." Ginny answered, looking from face to face.

"Let us get back home; she will be considered our property since we have found her."

"Wait a sec Erric. Shouldn't we give her our markings before we get home? I don't know about you, but I don't want to fight to keep her-we have been gone for a while and I just want to relax." Darr said.

"Alright, let's get it over with."

"What are you going to do?" Ginny asked with rising trepidation.

"Phen, drape her over Darr and hold her." Erric ordered.

"Wait; what are you going to do?"

"Hurry Phen, let's get this over with." Darr said urgently.

Ginny was thrown, none too gently, belly down over Darr's back. Her long honey blond hair touched the ground, blocking anything she could see except the underbelly of the horse man. She gasped when she saw a long thick phallus dangling beneath him. She wasn't sure what it was, but some internal instinct screeched at her that it wasn't something she wanted to know about. Before her thoughts could process, the swaths of gauzy material that covered her body, was thrown over her head, and a painful biting sensation pushed against her ass-cheek. She screamed and tried to buck away, but a set of hands held her immobile.

"Is the brand complete?" Phen asked.

"Just a bit longer, I want there to be no question to who she belongs." Erric said, pushing the small instrument tighter against her flank.

Ginny was shaking from the pain. Brand! They were branding her. She had read the scrolls describing brands used in different tribes and kingdoms, but never had she read about the stinging, fiery pain.

"Stop-stop-stop. Oh gods stop!" She screeched.

Finally, Eric pulled it away, but before she could gulp in much needed air, another brand, Phen's, pushed tightly against her other cheek.

"Where will you put yours Darr?" Erric asked. Darr chuckled and she felt the vibrations of his amusement beneath her.

"On her breast, hurry Phen." Darr warned.

Ginny's body shook from the pain, tears rolled down her cheeks, and she couldn't scream, because she couldn't draw in a breath. Phen pulled the instrument from her buttocks and she was quickly removed from Darr's body. Her lungs were burning, her mouth wide in horror, but still no breath came.

"Dammit! Erric, she's not breathing." Phen worriedly stated.

Darr grabbed her face and blew air into her starving lungs. She gasped in a lungful of air and a scream rushed out ending in choking sobs.

"Bare her." Erric urged.

She was draped over the large log she had hid under earlier. Hands grabbed her wrists from above and held her ankles below. Her raw backside burned from the material of her robes and the ruff bark beneath her. Darr parted the front of her coverings, her breasts spilling out and pointy from the chill of the air.

"Damn." Darr's hands cupped her breasts. His freakishly large hands couldn't hold in the voluptuous cleavage of her bosoms.

"Perfect! She will be successful in nursing our young." He claimed.

"Pick one." Phen ordered, having no problem keeping Ginny immobile. Ginny saw Darr pull off a long necklace that resembled silver. He cupped it in his hands and blew on it while keeping eye contact with her. His eyes glowed blue and when he pulled the necklace away, the end glowed a red hot horseshoe shape.

Ginny was shaking her head and whimpering words that even she couldn't make out. Darr had a look of regret etched in his features when he pressed the glow of the small thumb size print to her upper right breast.

"This is for your own protection. Females who are unclaimed do not live very long or happy lives with our kind. We are bestowing a mercy to you, by giving our brand." Darr said with his face close to her own.

Ginny's body tensed for the abuse and her body was too well pinned for her struggles to matter. Black spots overtook her vision, and she sank blissfully into unconsciousness.

Chapter 2: Their Virgin Union

Ginny's eyes opened to see a large room lit with torches. Fur caressed her naked body and she looked down to see it was some kind of animal skin. By the size of it, it must have been from a bears that she had learned about in the scrolls.

"How did you acquire a bride from the Rain Palace? I thought we were banned from their land nearly a century ago." Someone said asked?

Ginny closed her eyes to hide the fact that she was awake.

"The Arru'Feltons attacked the palace. She ran from them and ended up in our territory. We found her and branded her." It was Phen, she remembered that voice.

"Shit; is there an opening in your union?" The new voice asked.

"Sorry Zark, she doesn't look like she could handle more than the three of us." Erric said.

"You're probably right. Do you think there may be more females that escaped?" Zark asked with a note of anticipation.

"There might be, I doubt the Arru'Feltons were welcomed with open arms. Suppose we sent in a few of us to clear them out and claim the women as a payment to our efforts?" Darr said.

"And bring them back here, to discover their bellies rounded by their seed? I don't think so." Zark said with disgust.

"Send the unwanted babes back to the palace once it is restored. The male babes can go to next of kin from the women and the females can go to the palace for the Minotaurs. It is an even exchange for help. Times are obviously getting harder for the other clans and a new alliance with us and the mine people will protect the Rain Palace." There was a moment of silence after Erric spoke. Ginny could tell by their breathing, the words were being considered.

"I'll inform the other males of what I have learned today. Any in favor of the trade can either go or stay. The females won't be virgins of the old treaty made, but our numbers have never been lower than they are now. It would be nice to hear the whinnying of babes again." With those parting words, Zark left.

"It's alright Ginny; you can open your eyes. We know you're awake." Phen whispered by Ginny's ear.

Her eyes flew open in surprise not knowing Phen had settled himself so near her. Surely such a large body couldn't have moved so silently without disturbing her bed of furs? His arms caught hers and drew her up against his horse belly-between his front hooves and back. She let out a whimper from his heat and the fear of her predicament.

"Do you know what we expect of you sweetness?" Darr bent on his front legs to cup her cheek. She shook her head keeping eye contact.

"Do you remember us branding you?" Ginny froze up and nodded at the remembered pain from their first meeting.

"That's good." Her eyes widened, and Darr quickly spoke.

"Not from the pain; that wasn't good. It's good that you remember us binding you into a union with us. Erric; Phen, you, and I are now a union. Humans sometimes call it marriage and smaller clans call it 'bound' in another way to say it, bound to each other. Do you understand? We aren't certain what all you have learned at the time you spent at the palace, but maybe you could tell us after we eat."

Ginny hunched her shoulders as she sat on a makeshift chair. A thin leather thong collared her throat, with the tail of it falling down her back to reach her heels. They said it was a symbol of union, besides the brands. When the wounds healed, she would be permitted to wear clothing outside of their home with the collar adorning her neck. All claimed women wore them, apparently.

The three horsemen rested on their bellies with legs out from under them around the table. In front of her were a plate with roasted meat; berries, dried figs, cheese, and manchent bread. Phen, Erric, and Darr had already started eating and talking among themselves, all Ginny could do was hold herself and stare at the food.

A finger caressing her arm jerked her out of the stillness of her mind and she stared at Darr.

"Did you hear me Ginny?" She shook her head, Darr smiled, which softened his features boyishly.

The three had large plump lips and sturdy jaws, but they were still different in appearance; gorgeous.

"I asked if you were ready to tell us of your experiences in the Rain Palace; what have you learned?"

Ginny rubbed her arms covering her breasts that, no matter how hard she tried, were too large to be hidden. It angered her that they braided her hair back, to rest along her back so she couldn't hide herself from their gaze.

"We learned to read scrolls. Self-control of our feminine weaknesses and curious minds was a daily lesson."

"And what are these weaknesses and the curiosity that plagues the feminine minds?" Phen asked with a charming half smile.

"Talking, mostly; we took short term vows of silence and stillness. Our Dame instructor didn't tolerate babbling; giggling, snickering, laughing, or questions. She said a woman's most charming attribute was looking at a statue and perfecting its grace and its stillness." She looked around at their stunned silence and open mouths, she felt like a bug.

"Well she wasn't taught anything about pleasing a centaur union. They have instructed those females to be nothing but useless to us since they broke the treaty. And by the tone of her body, physical exercise wasn't on the list either."

"We walked the palace length every day putting our weight on the outside of our feet from heel to toe when barefoot and quietly in the special shoes. We also had to float in water on our backs." Ginny stuck out her chin a little. That was the biggest challenge she had. Learning to float in water until someone waded in to draw her out to the side without her flailing and getting water up her nose. She didn't like water, and took many sinking dunks in the dangerous depths.

"Well-uh, that's very…" Phen started to say but lost words and look to Darr to smooth over whatever he messed up saying.

"I bet you exceeded the expectations of grace and statue like qualities." Darr smoothed over.

Ginny beamed a smile that lit up her face and started to pick at her food. Erric; Phen, and Darr talked of tomorrow's agenda. When Ginny pushed her plate aside, all three horsemen stood and held out a hand.

"It is time to cement our union Ginny."

She held her hand out to Darr, whose expression was the most kind at the moment. Something foreign and scary blazed in Phen's and Erric's eyes, making them glow. She shivered a bit at their scrutiny and walked along with Darr down a wide hallway. He pushed open a door, and in the center of the room was a large and oddly shaped table. It was smooth and dark. There was a groove on top and on the sides were grooved inward and then flared back out a little bit.

Darr lifted her naked body and placed her in the center of the table.

"Lean forward Ginny." He gently placed his hand at the small of her back and pushed her forward so she lay on her belly. He adjusted her legs so they straddled the wooden furniture and her knees rested along the grooves.

Phen smiled when he stood by her face, with his hands propped where, if he were human his hips would be.

A hand ran down between the crevice of her ass and thighs. Her upper body shot up in surprise at the foreign touch. The palace had punishments reserved for intimate touches to a woman's own body.

"Relax sweetness, let us touch you, we are in a union now and it's perfectly acceptable." Phen said as he caressed her hair.

Ginny blew out a breath and lay back on her belly. Fear of the unknown notched up her pulse rate and she chewed on her lower lip. Two sets of hands touched; probed, and ran along her back; thighs, and pussy. She felt the familiar wetness of warm oils, but it wasn't rubbed into her muscles like was familiar; instead it was kneading between her thighs; up high in that secret place she never touched. She groaned when a finger moved quickly back and forth at her nubbin and warm shots of awareness went straight to her womb, clenching and creating a warm wetness deep inside of her.

"That's it, let it go love. Let it feel good." The husky voice of Erric rumbled behind her.

Ginny's hips moved toward the source of her newfound excitement to their own accord. Her mouth opened in awe and her eyes rolled back as her legs quivered and tightened on the table. Strange noises filled her ears and she knew it was from her, but the noises amplified when two fingers parted her folds and pushed inside. The sensation wasn't as good as before, but then they started moving in short strokes and wiggles.

"Yes!" She hissed between clenched teeth.

Something was building within her and it was going to be big. Whatever 'it' was; was something new and scary. Would she die? The building pressure within her felt almost painful, but so good at the same time. Phen held her wrists to the sides of the table, his thumbs circling softly at her wrists. Her eyes opened wide and she looked at him, her hips still jerking and shaking.

"H-help me." Ginny gasped out.

Phen smiled and brought one wrist to his mouth and he licked and drew patterns with his tongue. Suddenly, like a rope strung too tight, the building feeling within her snapped and Ginny writhed and her body jiggled all over from the explosive falling feeling deep inside her woman parts. She bellowed out sounds and her body started clenching and tightening again with the talented fingers touching her.

"She's ready." Erric announced with a gruff voice.

A dark shadow came over her, and she saw hooves in her peripherals settling on each side of her.

"Perfect fit."

A large wet bulbous knob bumped against her twitching pussy lips as she felt the belly of a horse above her. Hooves from beneath were clapping the floor, moving, which adjusted the knob to fit the hole of her woman's channel. Her searching eyes found Phen, who was watching with no small amount of lust looking into her eyes. He turned his body a bit and she focused on the long purple and pink cock hanging from under him. Her eyes went wider, then back to his face.

"It will feel really good if you let it." He whispered to her.

The cock kissing her pussy pushed in, meeting the resistance of her untouched channel. She gasped at the too full feeling just inside of her.

It wasn't stopping though. Deeper and deeper the long thick horse cock jerked in and out of her, until he paused.

"You won't be a virgin any longer." Erric said above her, and then thrust in hard heavy strokes.

Ginny felt like she was being ripped open and stretched impossibly wide. What made these half human beings think that this wouldn't permanently injure her? She made noises of distress and Phen talked to her in hushed tones.

"He's not even in all the way Ginny. Don't think of it as just a big cock inside of you, think about how in control Erric is and how he is being gentler to you because you're human." Ginny could only groan at Phen's distasteful words and the instruction bucking deep inside of her.

"Gods she's so tight, it's like an iron fist around my cock. Fuck! It hurts so good; Darr work her, I am losing control." Erric grunted.

Ginny could hear his hooves tapping against the floor and feel the strength he had over her. She was immobile and helpless, but for some reason that didn't bother her as much as it should have. Should it? Darr reached under her and played with her clit, back and forth, a fast staccato to Erric's rhythm. Heat and arousal bloomed within her once again and Erric hit a bundle of nerves within her that had her crying out in ecstasy and bucking against his protruding member.

"Ah-fuck-yes! So tight; so hot and wet Ginny." Erric grunted, his movements growing harder, his large balls slapping against her clit as she lifted herself onto her knees to move against him.

She felt so filled with him and he was pushing more and more at the very end of her. Her pussy clenched and unclenched as she felt small spurts of heat splashing against the inside of her, tingling and making nerve endings zing and explode with rapture. She was so close to that peak again and she no longer could make her body obey her commands.

"I'm going to come deep inside you Ginny." Erric grunted. "I will fill that tight little pussy up with my seed until you overflow, then Darr will fuck you before your sweet cunny misses my cock."

She felt his big horse cock flex and swell even more, then a forceful blast of semen burst within her. The impact of the life-giving liquid pushing inside of her was indescribable and amazing at the same time. She felt herself stretch even more from the pressure, and then he pulled out and backed away. She felt a heavy gush, her pussy expelling the liquid and it flowing like a raging river down her thighs, soaking the table beneath her, then Darr straddling himself around her and pushed deep inside without the careful slow strokes Erric had started out with. That did it for her, her pussy throbbed and clenched around him the second he was as far in as her body would allow and she flew over that peak, shaking and twitching. Her eyes rolled and her whole body seized in a maelstrom of raw heated pleasure. It was the perfect torture. Her own body gushed its release and Darr never let up. He was working himself in and out in a race for his own release.

"Fuck! Perfect fucking pussy. My cock is fatter than Erric's, you like me pounding you hard like this? Are you my mare, Ginny? Tell me you're my little mare."

"Yours! Your mare!" She screamed, still twitching and fighting to come down from the prolonged orgasm that clutched her body.

Her admission to being his brought Darr's climax full throttle. She was sliding along the table, in her own juices and Erric's, feeling someone pushing her back into the table to stop her from going over the end. Darr's fluids filled her like Erric's, making her feel ready to explode deep within. He yelled out his satisfaction and she thought she heard a horse-like nicker. His body shook and he backed his unsteady legs away from her. Feeling his girth slide from her clenching depths made another climax throb and pulse. She shook, she shivered, she screamed out.

Ginny was flipped over to lie on her back, her hips humping the air; lifting up and down, seeking to be filled and on the brink of another orgasm. The muscles in her legs stiffened and released, trying to come together and clasp, to put more pressure on her swollen, blood filled clit. Phen's face came into view and he smiled, showing beautiful white teeth and a golden goatee.

"Beautiful! So responsive, just the way I like 'em. Your sweet little pussy wants more, huh?" Phen asked.

Ginny couldn't respond. Her whole body was tingling and ready for more. Even her fingers shook and her skin was over sensitive. Her nipples felt hard and aching, she looked at them and Phen's gaze shifted to them.

"Oh you poor thing, you need a little loving; is that it? A little push to take you over the edge; your nipples are like ripe little berries and I love berries." His lips wrapped around the distended peek of one pink nipple and Ginny's weak screams were hoarse when she cried out. If he didn't let her come, she would die. She was dying now; dying for more, for less, for it to stop, to never stop.

"Please." She moaned out.

Phen nipped her gently, then swirled his tongue to lick the sting away. His lips traveled down her body, raising the raging fever building beneath her skin. He spread her thighs apart and wriggled his tongue side to side on her super sensitive clit.

"Look at that pretty little clit, so full and ripe, so responsive and begging for attention." Phen said aloud.

A finger and thumb gently pinched her clit and she bucked some more.

"I think our little filly could use some giddy-up gear, what do you think Darr?" Erric asked. Phen's finger plunged inside of her, smoothing her wetness and drawing it out.

"Maybe a bit and clit clamp."

"Not this time Erric, I need inside this sweet pussy. Fuck, I can't even wriggle my fingers she's clasping me so tight." Phen nearly groaned.

He moved up to straddle the table and his phallus bobbed in his excitement. It bumped against her slit, but kept sliding with how wet she had become.

"Ginny, reach down." Phen ordered.

Ginny's arm shook so badly as she reached down and for the first time felt a cock in her hand. He was hard, but smooth and rippled with veins. Her fingers wrapped around the cock that would soon be inside of her and noted how her fingers couldn't even touch. She guided the tip to her hole and cried out when Phen just forced his length inside of her much like Darr. Her back slid against the table and she lifted her legs to rest her feet against his hind horse legs, this gave her some leverage to work with and against him. Taking and giving what she wanted. Her hands went up around him and dug into his thankfully long coat of hair. She was mindless and so far gone, only thinking about coming one more time.

"Hold her hand down!" She heard Phen yell, as her hands were pulled flat to the table and her hips and legs worked up as his fast gate plowed down. It hurt! It hurt so much it felt good. The small fiery spurts of pre-come were super sensitizing her nerve endings making her cry; beg, and babble for completion.

"I'm not…gonna… last." Phen said as his speed doubled.

Before Ginny could grasp that much needed extra caress, Phen exploded with a cry deep inside, bucking the end of her and his deep sharps spurts of release overfilling and splashing out of her. When he pulled out and backed away, Ginny was still in need. Her hips still were gyrating and body tremors shaking her. Phen's mouth latched onto her swelled clit that was peeking out from between her pussy lips. He sucked in strong tugs and twittered his tongue beneath it. Her body froze up, ceasing all movement, and then she plunged from the high peek she had climbed. She screamed and she gushed out her release.

"Holy fuck man! Holy fuck, she's a squirter!" Darr said excitedly, his body prancing to show his excitement.

Ginny's own feminine ejaculation squirted all over Phen's face, and when he finally pulled away, she was still in the throes of her very special release.

"Oh baby." Phen whispered. "You are amazing and I can't wait to return the favor." He said in awe.

Three sets of hands ran along her body. Tamping her down, helping her relax and still. They mumbled sweet words of praise and appreciation, sending her smiles and bending to place delicate kisses wherever they could. Ginny's body went to sleep before her eyes closed, she couldn't move and she felt safe that her guys; her studs, would take care of her. This was the most calm she felt since the palace was under attack. A smile lifted her lips and she sighed in contentment.

Who would have ever thought my day would end like this? That thought flitted through her mind.

Story 2:

Chapter 1- Zark's Search

After seeing the naked human woman that his buddies; Darr, Phen, and Erric had claimed and formed a union with, Zark had informed the other stallions about the Rain Palace. He never waited for their opinions and quickly set out on a search for his own human girl. He hoped he didn't get one with a belly full of someone else's seed, but Erric's opinion to solve that problem was logical so as not to taint their bloodlines. Send the child, if there were to be one, off to the Minotaurs.

Zark had help strapping leather belts around him with attached bags of needed essentials. He had met human women before and knew they were always in high demand for one thing or another. He also didn't plan on sharing a female with any other males of his kind. He wanted one all to himself. Once he found her, he would brand and claim her immediately. His sexual need was high lately; lack of breeding had done that to him. There was a shortage of females at home, and he wouldn't ask for the right to breed and be rejected again. Oh-no! Not this time. He wanted to have his own female to plow without taking turns.

Zark set off on a determined canter, breathing in and out through his nose so he wouldn't tire quickly. The thought of breeding made his dick distend and thicken, but he forced the arousal back, not wanting to injure the sensitive flesh with the underbrush he was working through.

He stopped a few times, sniffing the air and staying within the bounds of their own territory. He hydrated often and refused to eat until after he was ready to rest. Night fell into morning by the time he reached the farthest northern boundary, now he would turn into hunting mode. His long white blond hair was braided back to dangle down his back, and his senses were honed for a female. He stepped lightly, avoiding noise and twigs. It was only fair to capture females who walked into centaur territory, everyone knew of the warnings stretched among the wooded lines.

Dust motes drifted out of Zark's path, creating a clear way for him. This land recognized him as he followed small bursts of sunrays along the forest floor. Wallow-jays, small birds with large mouths, twittered their morning tunes, communicating to each other in their loud ways. Zark smiled knowing the Wallow-jays were even now upset with his disturbance in their early morning chatter.

Walking on the very edge of the centaur land, Zark looked beyond the green fields claimed by human tribes. It had been nearly a century since his kind allowed themselves to possibly be seen this close to human lands, but he figured he'd be able to lure a female if she spotted him. They are a curious lot, those humans.

Zark stopped in his tracks when he heard a Shoo-shoo bird, which literally sounded like it was saying, 'Shoo-shoo'. Their human like phrase tricked the forest animals into thinking that a human was around and scared them off with their human like expression. Zark cocked his head to the side and listened. He heard footsteps up head and camouflaged himself into a thicker part of the brush. The footsteps came slowly closer; he counted in his head the steps; one, two, one, two. There wasn't an extra two steps following, letting him know it was a two legged creature instead of a four legged. He stayed quiet, to observe first.

"Laya, why won't you marry me? Your dad said it would be a perfect match and you won't have to clean-up after your brothers all day. Five brothers against one husband, wouldn't that sound much better?" A whiney male voice filled Zark's ears, followed by the sweetest female voice that flowed like music.

"Ha-ha, that's funny Thomas. Why would I want to leave my family home and go into servitude to another man who would have more authority over me than my brothers and father? My answer is still no." The female, Laya said with tinkling laughter lacing her voice.

"But why?" The whiney Thomas begged.

"I just told you; I don't want to be your cook; maid, or your bed partner. I have better things planned for my life and I only have to wait two more years before my father releases me from my maidenly obligations. I will be considered too old for a marriage contract or bargain then. I really couldn't be docile for you Thomas, go find a sweet girl that will gush and grovel under your feet, you're really barking up the wrong tree."

"Well you wouldn't have much choice if I had my way with you right now though. Your father would make you marry me." The annoying human male threatened.

Zark was ready to walk out and beat some sense into the male when he spotted the female with a blade pressed against the male's throat. By the gods, Zark was hard and nearly panting seeing this warrior woman defending herself. He would wait it out a little longer to see if she needed any help.

"Don't you ever threaten me Thomas; I will slice your throat where you stand and leave your rotting carcass for the centaurs to feed on. You only want me because I can hunt along with my training to be a wife. You are lazy and I will not lay beneath a man that I have to care for like a babe rooting for its mama's tit."

Laya leaned into Thomas with her best killing face to look him in the eyes. She saw fear and smelled piss. Looking down confirmed Thomas wetting himself in his britches, she smiled the cold hearted witch smile everyone at the village accused her of being and whispered loudly.

"Run." She said.

Thomas stumbled back, landed on his backside then ran back out of the forest, probably to tell her brothers and father she tried to kill him. Let him. She thought, her brothers would just laugh in his face and reward her with a new weapon or other.

"Stupid swine," she mumbled aloud. Laya walked on, enjoying the silence and early morning crispy air. She had no sisters and her mother quit trying to make her into a desirable bride by her nineteenth year, she was now twenty-one and proud not to be attached to a man. She had bigger plans for herself, reaching the goal of her own cottage her father had promised her by the time she turned twenty-two, if she were still unmarried. He agreed her dowry would be her own to live on and she would still have the protection of her family whether she agreed to it or not.

Laya stopped when she heard…nothing. Her hunter's instincts kicked in as she notched an arrow her father made to fit her perfectly. She was a tall woman, almost reaching the height of her brothers and was intimidating to most men; it was her advantage over them.

"I know you're there, come out where I can see you."

Zark was surprised that this warrior female could sense him, she was a fighter and he liked that a lot. He walked a ways toward her, still covered from the waist down with thick brush so she wouldn't see his horse half. His arms were raised high and he couldn't pack away the cocky smile that etched his features. His white blond hair was a beacon to her, he knew, but she would be able to tell right away that he wasn't an old human man since he was physically toned and still quite young.

"Who are you and what are you doing in the centaur forest? Don't you know that you risk your own life trespassing?" Laya said with a lethal tone to her voice. The man that stood off the path was gorgeous and tightened her belly with arousal.

"I could ask the same of you. Aren't you afraid of risking your own life walking these woods?" Zark replied.

"No."

"No? Why ever not?"

She had taken him by surprise and his confusion sounded in his voice.

"Because I am a woman."

"And? How is your gender a factor in the trespasser's fate?" Zark cocked his head at the tall woman with a head full of brown curls.

"My grandmother claimed that centaurs have no use for a dead woman." She said blandly.

Zark scratched the back of his neck. What else could he say? She was right.

"I like your bow, may I see it?" He asked.

Laya's eyes narrowed on the attractive man. Did he think her a simpleton?

"Are you stupid, or do you think me daft? I assure you I am not the later, so you must be the first." She growled. Heavens help him, but she turned him on.

"Come out onto the path slowly."

"I have met many simple minded females and was just curious to know how you compare. I am not moving from this spot, howbeit you come this way?"

"Ha; and I'll start saying my own death speech. No thank you. What are you doing here?" Laya asked again.

"Do you want the truth?" Zark asked.

"That would be an excellent start."

"Lower your weapon and I will tell you." He watched her lower the bow to a position that wouldn't be a kill shot. He took a breath and launched himself with all the power his equine ancestors bestowed him, and took her by surprise. His arms wrapped around her, avoiding the arrow that flew and had her arms safely pinned to her sides. Her mouth was open in surprise, and he smiled down into her eyes. She was less than a head shorter than him and he squeezed her flush against the front of his body.

"I am a centaur, my name is Zark. You are trespassing and are now mine. First mistake was entering our boundaries; second mistake…" He lowered his face until their noses touched. "was lower your guard. Never lower your guard."

He growled the last in triumph and kissed her to seal the deal. Still kissing her, he secured one arm tightly around her body and reached to tiny pouch strapped around his torso. Inside, he pulled out a thorn with a sleeping solution smeared on the tip and poked it into her hip. She cried out into his mouth, then her body went lax in a deep sleep that would last only hours. He made quick work of divesting her of her weapons and hidden ones at that; then bound her with ropes and gagged her. Securing her, belly down, on his back was a little tricky without help, but he managed and spirited her away before anyone else decided to come along.

Miles away, deeper into the forest, he laid her down and pulled her shirt to the side to reveal her upper arm. He felt a great urgency to brand her now, knowing she wouldn't take kindly to him if she were awake. He blew on his silver horseshoe necklace until it was iron hot and pushed it against her upper arm. He held it tightly, thankful that she was still in a deep sleep and wouldn't feel the pain. Moments ticked by until he was sure the mark would be permanent and he carefully slung her across his back. He had many more miles and hours to travel before he could safely claim her, he was still too close to the borders where humans were known to occasionally roam.

It was later in the day, closer till nightfall when he made camp and waited for her wake. A small fire burned with roasted rabbit and a small helping of dried fruit and a flask of water. She moaned from the effects of the drug he forced into her body and he didn't until now have second thoughts about removing the gag. He felt sure she would have a few negative things to say to him. When her dark brown eyes opened, he knew when memory surfaced, because the killing look she sent his way almost-almost made him regret his decision to keep her.

He couldn't fight the smile that bloomed on his face when she growled at him. She lay on her side, still effectively bound with the ropes he had brought for this journey.

"Hi." He said.

"I am going to kill you." She promised. She was so cute, he thought.

"Thanks for the warning. I told you my name is Zark, right? And your name is Laya. I made some food because I knew you would be hungry." And as if on cue, her stomach chose that moment to grumble.

"I'll hand feed you since you are tied up nice and tight for the moment."

"I am really going to kill you once I get out of these ropes." She said with a steely voice.

"Uh-huh. Let's sit you up so you can take a drink." He positioned her upright, and tilted the flask to her lips.

She refused to open and water dribbled down her chin.

"Oh come on, it's just water." He tilted it to his lips for a sip, and then swallowed. "See?" Then put it back to her mouth.

He waited and smiled when her lips parted to the opening for a healthy swallow. Timid little thing, he thought. She probably concluded he would trick her again and she was right, he would. He liked feisty females and knew how to handle them. When she turned her head away, to signal she was done, he took a bite from the roasted rabbit then fed her with his own hands. With every bite she took, he had to move his hand away quickly because she was determined to take a finger or two each time. The light from the fire enhanced her dark beauty and shone brightly in her eyes.

"So now that is out of the way, we can work on other hungers." He tossed her a cheeky smile that the centaurian women sighed over.

"I am going to kill you." She repeated. Zark wouldn't let her words frazzle him; he was too happy a centaur for that to happen.

"And a lovely night it is; now, onto better things." He heaved his large equine body to a stand and pulled her up after himself. He smiled down into her beautiful face and couldn't stop his body from prancing for her notice. His tail lifted up in a show of his stallion maleness and his hind legs stomped.

Laya wouldn't show her fear, her father always taught his children to never show their fear or weaknesses to an enemy. She was sure by the way his body moved around that he was in a high state of arousal. She had seen how the farm horses and warrior horses pranced and danced for the pretty mares in heat and she had a moment of 'oh-fuck-I'm-screwed' drift through her mind. What a mean twist of fate that his human half was so gorgeous. It was the animal part of his anatomy that almost had her begging for mercy and balling like a babe.

"I am going to enjoy and cherish every moment we have together Laya. I am worthy of you. I desire no woman to be my keeper. I hunt my own food and only want a woman who will stand beside me, a strong woman who isn't afraid to fight when needed, someone to pass the lonely nights with. And…" His white smile widened even farther, almost…almost enchanting her. "you will lie beneath me, because it is the only way." He added softly, knowing he would get a rouse out of her. The little spitfire ground her teeth and he saw a fire of her own light her dark eyes.

"I am going to kill you, slowly." She got out between gritted teeth. Zark through back his head and bellowed his laugh. His silvery blue eyes were full of mirth when he looked back into hers.

"We are making progress; you can now put together seven words."

"Very. Slowly." She huffed.

"I think you will change your mind once we get home, I plan on loving you up until you no longer have that desire. You will be saying other things like," his voice hit a higher pitch, mimicking a female voice. "Oh Zark-yes, more-more! Don't stop, uh-uh ooh Zark!'"

"Enjoy your laughter now horseman, you're already dead and just won't lie down." she growled.

"See? I knew you had a broader vocabulary." He bent her over a log he had hauled in and fixed earlier, quickly untying her legs and re-tying them to straddle the log after quickly hauling her male pants off one leg. She had squirmed and bucked, but she was no match to his strength. Saucy little wench, he thought. He walked over to the log, straddling it himself, then with even more speed, fixed her hands until they were tied around the log with very little wiggle room.

He slapped her ass lightly when profanities spewed from that lovely mouth and she yelped then turned her head so she could shoot a killing glare at him.

"My, my if looks could kill," he said as he pinched then rubbed her rosy ass-cheek.

"I am going to kill you." She said again.

"Back to that are we? Well, let's save your sweet words for later while I do this."

She gasped when his fingers rubbed up and down on the slit of her vagina. She had never let a man touch her there before and his warm fingers were starting to pull a foreign reaction from her.

She scolded herself mentally for the tingles she was starting to feel. No! no, you moron, this doesn't feel good. Think of something else, ya like Daddy's smelly feet and my brother's bed sheets. Ya-think of that. That feels good. What? Oh my gods that feels good. No! No it doesn't. Don't think about what his fingers are doing, don't think about that glorious flicking-oooh! Right there.

Laya waged war on an inner battle, not wanting to acknowledge the things Zark was doing to her body. Her hips pushed back for a deeper caress and she groaned at her feminine weakness. She felt humiliated and defenseless and was sure he would laugh at her reaction. Hot breath fanned her ear.

"Right there?" He whispered in a husky voice, no laughter etched in it at all. In fact, he sounded aroused and utterly serious. She risked a look at his face as she felt damp heat coat his fingers. His eyes were darker and his plump lips were parted.

"You feel so good Laya. Truly, you cannot possibly be of this world."

Oh-curse his tongue and sexy words! Little whimpers escaped her throat, as one finger pushed inside of her and moved around with practiced skill. Her head flung back as her legs clamped tightly around the log.

Zark walked around log so it was to his side, he was now facing her very delectable rear. He parted her soft globes with his hands and pulled her hips up a little, without causing strain on the ropes. He bent his head down to taste her female nectar that now coated his fingers, he couldn't help himself, he just needed to taste her. One swipe of his tongue from her woman's passage to clit wasn't enough. He groaned with her intoxicating scent and taste on his tongue and wriggled his mouth more. He latched onto her clit and sucked in deep pulls with his talented mouth. The little bud was distended and begging for release. When he worked it into a perky pink that peeked out from between her folds he released the tasty nubbin. One more swipe and an open mouth kiss, he settled for watching two of his fingers work inside of her like magic. He controlled the movements by her breathing patterns and soft husky sounds, working more of the white pearly drops from inside of her.

Laya lay there helpless to the onslaught of sensations the beast-man provoked from her body. She no longer felt humiliation, but excitement; she was itching to see it through all the way to the end, whatever that may be lead. She opened her eyes and saw the white body of the horseman and the very large erection he sported. Oh-gods, that's too big! She inwardly wailed. He will split me in two. His long fingers were moving faster now, making her jerk and twitch to get away; to get closer, to do something. His cock bobbed and flexed. Mid-way up, it actually bent in a slight curve, reaching his stomach.

Laya groaned again. His cock was lighter shades of blue, purple, and pink. It was disgusting, and yet arousing. What will it feel like? She wondered. It will feel like a bloody battle ax you MORON! She screamed to herself. His body pranced away from her, his tail lifted and flicking back and forth. Zark's fingers moved deeper within her channel and his thumb pressed snuggly on her clit, circling and coating it with her own juices. Her eyes shut as a strong clenching in her womb begun and made her fly off a peak of colors and wild sensations.

She screamed out in pleasure, as more of her fluids coating her pussy, and then she felt the belly of horseflesh move up her back. How did she get turned around so fast? Hands clasped the log above her as the head of his cock probed her slit. It was already slimy with his lubricant and Laya felt the quivering thickness dance in jerky movements at her hole. He didn't just enter her; he teased and flexed the thick mass of his wide cock head. A bit further in, it would kiss, then circle, tease her clit, then probe a bit further. She was a twitching mess of anticipation, fear, arousal, and curiosity. She was so wet and slick that she wondered how he could control where he wanted it to go. The head was worked inside, but didn't exit, instead stayed in with slow deliberate movements. She sucked in a breath when she heard Zark groan in…pleasure?

Frustration? Pain? A little bit more and he was working his girth inside of her, touching nerve endings she had never known before. A more forceful thrust had her crying out in discomfort as he pushed through her maiden head and he froze.

"Laya?" He said her name with concern. She whimpered a little when his throbbing horse cock flexed. He pushed in more in controlled strokes. "Shit, you're so tight." A harder thrust. "Wet." Another hard thrust. "Hot." He rammed harder against her hitting the very end of her and stayed there a moment, letting her adjust to his size. He angled the rest of his cock that had no room to enter her and her hips tilted back, so that it rubbed her engorged clit, making her fight to feel it some more. It shot sparks of pleasure through her body and Zark kept a skillful rhythm and restrained strokes he made for her pleasure.

"Perfect." He gritted out. "I knew you would be." He groaned. Zark knew he had something; someone special that he would never be able to let go. This female, his mate would be the death of him if he ever lost her. She was his perfect match in all ways. He was fighting his instincts to keep this all for her, her pleasure, that's all that mattered. He would walk through a Pegasus army for her, if she only asked. He would march through the deserted lands above the Minotaur mines and into their leaky-cold caverns if she wished it. Zark was swimming in a burning pool of pleasure.

He jutted in and out, rubbing his lubricated shaft along her puckered clit and reveling in the sway of her hips and sing-song moans. He needed her to reach her peak soon, before he lost control. His release was clawing its way through his spine and gripping his balls to a near painful clench. Sweat beaded his brow and fell from his temple. Just a little. Bit. More. He told himself.

Laya rolled her hips without thought, getting closer and closer to another one of those free-falling feelings, like jumping from one of the cliffs into the deep blue waters; only this was better.

Her toes were curling and the sweet musky smell of horse; leather, man, and Zark was imprinting inside her brain, turning her on even more. His grunts and groans, made her feel powerful and womanly. Despite being tied to a log, she felt like she had some unknown power over him, giving him the pleasure he was experiencing. It was ever so good for her ego.

"Come for me Laya, let me feel you go wet and hot around my cock."

She bucked and writhed a little bit more, her clit rubbing stiffly against his phallus and she saw stars. Light exploded behind her eyes, and she shook from the force, crying out in rapture, in pleasure, in need. Wetness from her, coating the thick cock, making her gasp in surprise at what her body was capable of.

"Thank the gods!" Zark growled.

Gone with the steady sensual rhythm; gone with the shorter jerky movements; gone went Zark's mighty control. Her orgasm was drawn out with Zark's powerful beastly thrusts. Vigorous was he, to find and lose control. He powered into her like a battering-ram, tapping her cervix and charging her up for another peaking. A hot dribble of pre-come expelled from the tip of his thick cock, touching and caressing nerve endings and making small explosions lighting up and ricocheting deep inside. Her womb clenched, her pussy twitched, her walls clamped tight around him, releasing more of her own fluid and desperate to milk the seed from his cock. She cried out in ragged euphoria, followed by his shout of release. Hot blasts of semen scalded the walls of her vagina, the pressure almost painful, making her feel bloated down there.

His short jerky movements would have powered her from the log if she hadn't been tied down. Finally he stopped moving and just held himself, deep inside of her, prolonging the feeling of fullness, like he wanted it branded inside her head that this was not over; this would happen again and she would never crave another's touch. Slowly, he pulled his bobbing, slowly softening, dick out of her pussy and a rush of his seed deflated her as it gushed from her body and ran down her legs. His big horse body shivered as he back up and his human arms surrounded her as he kissed and rubbed her down. He was helping her down from that high, in slow deep caresses.

"Shhh." He whispered against her neck. Only then did she realize that she was whimpering as her body writhed then occasionally twitched from the after effects of so many powerful orgasms. "Oh Laya you are so perfect, in every way."

Laya closed her eyes and let her body go limp as the heat from his warm hands seeped into her muscles. Sleep had claimed her and she didn't bother to fight, she was content to let him care for her.

Chapter 2: Welcome Home

Zark had pricked her again with another thorn with a sleeping solution bathed on the tip; he wanted to get home with his female and away from any possible danger. He had taken advantage of the extra time he had to bath her and strip away the offending male attire she had worn on their first meeting. Clearing his large room of any possible weapons, he chained her ankle to the floor with plenty of room to use the relieving bucket. He set her clean naked body on the furs he had made into a bed on the floor and used the spare room to rest for himself. It had been a long couple of days, though to Laya it would only feel like one. He needed undisturbed sleep, safely away from her promise of killing him. He chuckled as he closed his eyes, knowing his spitfire would most likely kill him, and then ask for the key to her shackles.

Laya's head felt stuffy and she ached in so many places. She opened her eyes to see a skin of water, and a platter of food near her. Everything came back to her, realizing nothing was a dream. Dammit!

She chugged the water from the skin, and filled her grumbling belly with cold roasted meat and cheese. It would do, she had lived on worse during hunting trips and scout parties.

"Hello!" An unfamiliar voice called out. Laya stood and didn't shy away from her nudity when the tell-tale clomps of hoof beats walked toward the door of her room. "Zark!"

"Oh! Well hey there pretty lady, are you lost?" A centaur with shorn black hair leaned his human half against the over-sized door frame with arms and front legs crossed.

"Ya totally lost; because it just so happens that you see a naked woman chained to a floor every day." Her voice dripped sarcasm and promise menace.

The male's eyebrows shot up, and a small smile appeared.

"Huh I guess that means you really haven't been around here very long."

"I am going to kill you." She glared at him.

"Don't let her hurt your feelings Ryder; she says that all the time. It's just Laya's way of saying 'hi'." Zark clapped Ryder on the shoulder and walked down the hall, refusing to acknowledge Laya's presence.

"Oh-well then, it's nice to meet you Laya. Zark and I need to go have a talk so if you'll excuse me from your lovely self, I'll talk to you another time." Ryder said to Laya. He turned to go, and then pointedly looked back at her. "Don't go anywhere, you hear?" He winked and disappeared down the hallway.

Laya screamed in a blinding rage and chucked her plate where his head was less than a second ago. She missed, obviously, but was too angry to calm down, so she paced what the chain allowed her to pace.

Laya had worked herself into such a tither that she fell asleep again. She was having a dream of floating on white silk and tinker-flies floating down from their treetop perches to plant kisses along her face. Her lips formed a smile as she welcomed their attentions to her. She reaches out to gather the white silk closer so she could nuzzle and run it along her body.

"That's it Laya." A familiar voice grumbled by her jaw. She didn't stop to think why it was so familiar, because a pleasant flickering ran circles around her clit. She arched closer to the source and moaned from the tightening feeling deep inside of her.

"So pretty." That sexy voice said closer to her lips. She smelled apples on his breath when soft buttery lips took hers and swallowed her pleasure.

Zark knew it was a long shot to arouse her, but he had already decided that he would take her any way he could have her. He started with slow, soothing kisses, covering her face. He had bathed in the river earlier, so his hair was loose and dry, from running back home. It draped over both of them, closing them inside a white wispy haven. His fingers trailed down her warrior belly, memorizing every muscle and curve until he reached her swollen pearl tucked between amber curls, like a flower.

He knew the instant she was awake, her eyes fluttered and shock shown in her eyes as she looked at the fistfuls of hair clenched in her dainty hands.

"What are you doing?" She tried to sound mean, but it came out as breathy moans.

"Loving; adoring, and worshipping your body. You bring me to my knees Laya. You are the perfect female in every way." Zark whispered between kisses and little licks.

"I am going to kill you."

He lifted himself away and beamed an amused smile down at his little warrior. Had any female made him smile so much?

"But if you killed me, my sweet Laya, you wouldn't feel this again." He buried two fingers inside of her and moved them with speed, hitting all the good spots that made her writhe and twist.

"Trust me when I tell you, Horseman, one day you will be chained and at my mercy." She reached down his belly which was facing her side and grasped his distended cock. "And you may not find any pleasure." She meant for it to be a threat, but curiosity at the massive flesh in her hands had her exploring. Zark groaned and still kept up pushing his fingers inside of her and touching that sensitive bundle of nerves. They were both panting, challenging each other, fighting not to give into the throes of completion first.

Laya's hand moved all around his cock, feeling the blood pulsing in his veiny shaft. A small trickle of white liquid dribbled from the head, and cupped her hand on the bulbous head to smooth the moister over his cock. Amazement sprung through her when she noticed how he was putty in her hands. His body language and the groans coming from him turned her on more and more. She could not let herself climax before him, she wanted to force his on to prove her control and own dominance.

Zark was coming undone under her touch; it had been so long since he had been caresses. He knew the inner battle she waged and he could be accommodating. He would let her think she had the upper hand, it wouldn't get her very far or promise her freedom, but he knew his little warrior didn't like to feel helpless. He felt his seed boiling in his balls, and them drawing up tight against him. He kept his body still so as not to accidentally kick and injure her in his equine excitement. He slowed his touch on her to easy soft movements, giving her the lead in this joust of pleasure.

His cock stiffened and swelled and he groaned in the splendorous almost pain her flesh caused to his own. He felt his release rising in his shaft until it burst in hard pulsing streams on her hands, flowing down her arms and shooting all over her belly. He pulled her into his arms as his seed kept coming and he held her while he shuddered and groaned to the very last spurt, and then shivered.

He smiled then looked into her eyes ready to kiss and thank her for what she gave him, but one look in her eyes made his own confusion save the smile for later.

"Why do I see anger in your eyes Laya?"

"Let go of me." She growled out.

He shook his head. "No. I want you to tell me what has you so full of rage right now."

"You." She accused.

Zark was confused, and when she wiggled, he let her go. She stood to her full impressive height and he did as well. She whipped the furs apart wiping her body of his milky release. What had her so upset? She wanted him to climax first, he knew this, and granted her that small unspoken request. She was breathing hard and he came over to her to look into her eyes. He was shocked when he saw tears. He didn't even see tears when he first took her, whatever he did wrong must have really hurt her. He looked over her body, looking for any bruises or cuts his hooves may have caused.

"Did I hurt you Laya? I don't see anything. Talk to me beauty, do you hurt?" He couldn't stop the concern that made his voice tremble.

"I hate you." She said softly. Zark's hearts stopped and nearly broke from those three words.

"Laya…" He didn't know what to say. He fell to his knees as his hands gripped her hips and he bowed his head to her belly. "Laya, w-what…"

"Get away from me you bastard." She said with tears rolling down her face.

Zark would not give in. He wanted her too much to give up. Not only did he brand and start their union, it was entirely possible his seed took root deep in her womb. He shook his head and steeled himself from the venom of her words. He stood up and crossed his arms.

"We will stay like this until you tell me what I did wrong to deserve such harsh words." He said with a hard voice.

Laya was shaking with a burning fury that raced along inside of her. How could he act so clueless about how he treated her? It was bad enough that he branded her and oh-boy she didn't forget about that, fucked her and kept her chained to the floor. But did he have to come all over her like some common whore looking for coin? Did he have to cover her body with his fluids? She felt ashamed of herself and humiliated. She had higher expectations of him than him treating her like-like a chamber pot.

"You dumped yourself over me, like a bedside pot full of human waist." Her voice broke into hiccups then tears came down her cheeks.

Zark's mouth opened and shut, when nothing came out he engulfed her in his arms. He understood her now, she felt as if he humiliated and marked her; proving in a primitive beastly way his control over her. That wasn't the case and she would hear him out.

"Oh, Laya, Laya, Laya. It wasn't intentional at all, your hands felt so good touching me, and I had no ability to do anything else. I wasn't even thinking about the results, only that I didn't want you to stop touching me." He rubbed her shoulders and concluded that he didn't like his warrior female feeling beat down; he liked her fighting and sparring with him. "I meant nothing by it sweetness; I scared to move around, worried that I would hurt you. Come…let's go bathe."

"But you already bathed, I could tell when you came in."

Zark smiled down at her. "Laya, I would give anything to run my hands along your body. The fushia fish are in season and are in mass amounts of plenty, would you like to go fishing with me? We could also go hunting if you don't want fish."

Laya's mouth opened and closed in shock. He would allow her to keep her hunting skills in use? He had no problem with that?

"What is it Laya?" Zark asked with concern.

"It's just…" She looked into his magnificent blue silver eyes. "You want me to hunt and fish? It doesn't bother you?" Zark threw his head back and laughed his mirth. He looked into her surprised face and laughed again, holding her close to his body.

"What would make you think I want a docile union with a female only worried about house chores and how she dresses? Centaurs are a warrior race and all within are taught to defend and fight. I do not feel comfort in the possibility of me having a hunting accident or going to war without returning and you not being able to care for yourself. There are males here that would gladly take you into their home and form a union with you, but if you could care for yourself, you wouldn't feel obligated to be in a possible unwanted union." He paused for a moment, fury entering his eyes.

"I do not like thinking about another male touching you, or you welcoming another. It makes me very angry and full of rage to contemplate that. Call me selfish, but I do not want you to find comfort in the arms of anyone if I went to the afterlife." His hands tightened on her arms. "Do you understand me Laya?"

"I understand." Then she smiled. "I like hunting and fishing. I like the freedom of men's pants and riding astride, I do not like being kept indoors for long periods of time." She ended with a frown.

Was there ever a female, a human at that, so perfect for Zark?

"Come." He held his hand to her after he had given her a long swath of fabric to wrap around herself.

Chapter 3: The River

The river had a cold bite to it, when Laya jumped in without first testing the waters. She never saw the point in easing in slowly. Zark walked in after her head broke the surface and he led her to sit on his back.

"Would you give me a rub down fair Laya? Wash my back and I will wash yours." He had growl to his voice.

Laya laughed and positioned herself to rub his human portion with her strong fingers digging into his muscles. The water rested above her naval as she sat there kneading him. She watched the different fish swim by and heard the tell-tale signs of a 'Hoo-Gee' bird, birthing an egg. Which were a delight to have for breakfast anytime. They were interesting creatures and small; pushing an egg from their bodies nearly twice their own weight and size.

"Hello, hey…Zark!" Laya's head whipped to her right as she saw two female centaurs trotting into the clearing. One had blond hair and the other black. They were beautiful and both easily cleared fifteen hands.

"Elda, Peg! Come meet Laya." Zark waved them over. Laya felt jealousy swarm through her body, burning along her veins. How well did Zark know these strumpets? Did he mount them?

"Oh! You've got…you've got yourself a human." The pretty black haired said staring in disgust.

"She's simply…adorable." The blond turned her attention back to Zark. They waded into the clear water coming closer. Laya dismounted and swam to the opposite side for sheet to cover her nakedness. After securing it, she turned back to see Elda and Peg running their hands along his body. Laya saw red. She looked down at her feet and saw the leather straps Zark usually had secured to his body and found a knife sheathed along it. She snatched the knife and left, going back to Zark's home without him. She mentally stabbed him with his own weapon, letting the pain of other females touching him fulfill her inner tyrant.

At Zark's home, she found clothes similar to the ones she wore before her capture and with few alterations, she hid her knife and paced Zark's large abode. Her long dark hair was dry by the time she heard the clip-clop of horse hooves, then the large double doors slam open.

"Laya! Why did you run off? I have been searching everywhere for you, I thought you ran away. Explain yourself." Zark said with his arms crossed. His hair was braided back and she wondered which woman took the time to run their fingers through his silky tresses.

"Apparently you didn't notice my departure soon enough, if you had time to decorate and braid your hair." She did not miss the beads plated in to smaller braids near his ears.

"Elda and Peg offered to help." He shrugged, like it was no big deal. Oh she would show him it was no big deal, all in good time. She huffed and wet back to the room she had been sleeping in, making sure to lie upon the furs that hid her stolen knife.

"Well? Aren't you going to explain yourself?" He leaned against the doorway that held no door. Laya shrugged and tried for nonchalant.

"I am worn out and tired."

Zark nodded at that simple explanation, like it was reasonable. Oh Man! He had no clue. She had pride dammit. What was all of that horse-shite about him not wanting another man to touch her? Did that make it alright for two mares in heat to rub and prance around him? Not in Laya's world.

"I am tired as well." He walked in and lay beside her gently. She evened out her breathing and let a small smile tilt her lips when Zark had fallen to sleep. She waited a while longer, in case it was a trap, and then pulled the dagger from beneath the furs. With her free hand, she gripped his long thick braid, and with the other, sliced through it skillfully with the dagger. His hair barely touched his shoulders now, which made her a little sad, but humor threatened to bubble over in laughter when she saw how quickly his hair curled like pig's tails. She rolled out and donned his braid like a sash, if he didn't understand some of her female issues, like other grabby women, then he would have to learn by experience.

She had time to build a fire and fry the fish Zark brought back in his satchel before she heard his bellow of fury. She felt a little fear, but pushed it in the back of her mind, because she wouldn't back down from a bossy-egotistical man. Serves him right for letting those women touch him.

Serves him right for barreling through the door, demanding to know why she left without his 'by your leave'.

"Laya!" Zark stood between the hallway and the dining hall with his hands fisted at his sides, and his face an angry red. His eyes were swirling and his hair curled and puffed like silver pig's tails all over. She tried to hold it in-she did, but she couldn't. She bellied over in body wracking bellows of laughter. Tears of mirth ran down her cheeks and when he slowly stepped closer to her, the laughter started all over again. She ended up lying on her side, her ribs paining her from the bout of humor she was suffering. Eyes shut, nearly out of breath from constant giggles, until she heard the swoosh of a blade slicing her own hair.

She stood up and ran her hands along the butchered ends that fell just her shoulders, and cringed when her own hair curled like the tails of pigs. They stood and stared at each other for long silent moments.

"That was un-called for." She said between gritted teeth. Zark touched his head.

"Why would you think that? You moody heathen? You sliced through my hair while I was asleep, then" He pointed to her silver sash of hair; "wear it like a war flag. Tell me how I had no right!" He demanded.

"You let those mares touch you! While I was right there to witness it. They did your hair; you let them and welcomed their hands. You didn't even know I had left! Then-then you storm in here wondering-no, demanding to know why I had left. If you couldn't figure it out on your own, then it would have done no good telling you."

"Yes it would have! All you had to do was say something"

Laya screamed at him, not letting him finish whatever else he was going to say.

"So you could laugh at me and my feelings? So you could find humor at my expense then mount me and pretend my feelings don't matter? You go off blathering about other men-pardon, males touching me, but I have to suffer knowing other females can touch you? Sorry Zark, I am not that kind of woman. If I'm yours, then you're mine, and I will shear your hair to your scalp before I let you think others can run their hands along your body." Laya was fuming, mad and on the verge of finding a battleax and going on a spree.

The realization of his Laya's jealousy struck Zark like lightening. Beautiful! She was simply beautiful when she was close to feral. He saw her logic and decided to cool her rage before they both got too out of control. He would let her win.

"You are correct." He bent down on his front legs and bowed his head. "I am sorry Laya; I did you a great disservice and will not repeat my wrong doings again." He put a remorseful expression on his face. "Will you forgive me Laya? I am new to our union as well, but I beg you to not hold it over me."

Laya was stunned. Not ever, in all of her life, had a man ever admitted he was wrong and she was right. She expected any number of punishments from him besides him cutting her hair: a beating, a lashing, starvation, confinement…

"You're…you're sorry?" Laya asked with a small voice.

"To the very bottom of both my hearts; my sweet; you own both of them in the palm of your tiny warrior hands." He lifted his palms up in surrender. Laya ran to him and wrapped her arms around him to hold him close to her and shower his face with kisses. This union could work. He hadn't hurt her, physically. He had put her needs before her own and submitted to her when any other man, human or beast, would stomp their feet and keep fighting. Zark wasn't weak, but he obviously knew when to back down to Laya.

Zark carried her off to another room, with a large deformed looking table. He lay her down and divested her clothing with speed. Zark wrenched her legs apart and worshiped her body with his mouth, tongue, and fingers. Oh he is the perfect man. Laya thought.

He licked; nibbled, probed, and sucked along her woman parts with love and attention, never letting up when the pleasure became too much. He just kept going. A climax took her by surprise, her womb clenching in delight, and she screamed from the free-falling feeling. A furry underbelly brushed up along her own body, she turned her head and look down between them to the bobbing cock rubbing along her inner thighs, searching for her entrance. She reached down, clasped his prick, and guided it to her opening. She cried out when he just rammed in as far as her body allowed, nothing slow about this love play.

She bucked as he rammed, feeling her juices coating him, her pussy walls clenching him with wild abandon. Laya felt the little spurts of his pre-come, igniting her nerve endings, making her crazy for more. The liquid warmth heated her to incoherent babbles and the force of his penetration caused her legs to wrap around his soft belly for his easy access. She clenched her thighs as another wave of need rushed through her and the orgasm had her gasping for breath. Zark's ministrations became faster and without rhythm, his release when it came, shot deeply inside of her, stretching her further to near bloating. She pressed her hand above her pubic bone, feeling how full she was. She pressed harder and their fluids squirted from around his cock down her thighs, soaking her. Both of them belted their satisfaction to a near deafening pitch. Laya saw spots along her vision and gave into sleep.

When Zark backed off, he pulled her into his arms, and staggered to a pile of furs nearby. Still cradling his beloved, he not-so delicately plopped down, his legs buckling from beneath him. His lips quirked from the best breeding experience of his life. Oh he could get addicted to letting her win their small battles. His will is strong, but it was worth letting her win if he could mount her like this every time.

"Good morrow neighbors-ohhh!" Laya groaned at the familiar voice intruding their slumber. Ryder! She pulled Zark's dagger from the leather belt around his torso and flung it to the doorway near his head.

"Go away; we're not done our sleep." She snuggled back into Zark's warmth, ignoring the vibrations of his laughter.

"Dear me Zark! She is boar in the morning. And what in the hoof happened to your hair? What happened to her hair?"

"Does he never heed warnings?" Laya mumbled into Zark's chest. Another rumble of laughter answered from beneath her cheek.

"A slight misunderstanding Ryder, all is well. All is well indeed. You may want to flee before my Laya uses your hide as our wall décor, I couldn't stop her this morning; she has drained all my strength." Zark said to his friend.

"Feisty, huh? You got any more room for another in your union?" Ryder asked cheekily.

Before Zark could warn his lifelong friend of how dangerous his words were, Laya jumped up and surprised him with her mighty war cry. She had somehow pulled another dagger from him without his knowing and she was charging through their home, hot on the centaur's heels. Zark caught her before she could leave the yard in her naked state, and tossed her over his shoulder. He looked toward his neighbors home to see the very surprised and interested faces of Ginny, Darr, Phen, and Erric back from the watering hole; by the looks of them anyhow.

"She hasn't eaten breakfast yet." Zark hollered and waved at them, then ran back into his home with his warrior female and greet her proper good morning. "Nosy neighbors." He grumbled.

Across Zark's home, Faallen observed the commotion of the morning. A human female worth ten warriors, ready to attack Ryder, one of their best fighters. Interesting! Faallen thought to himself. He had been silently observing the submissive Ginny and her polar opposite, Laya since their arrival. Faallen was now very interested in what other types of human females were out there begging to be claimed, like these two. Maybe it was time for his search. He looked in the reflecting glass at his scarred and bulky appearance. Would a human female find me lacking? Will she scream in fear and disgust? Faallen shook his head and tossed aside the thought of having his own union. Even the centaur females avoided him, what would possess him to think any female would consider him a worthy mate?

The End

Thank you for reading. I hope that this quick fix-read helps all of those ladies out there who just want to grab their man and throw them on the bed and ride them like a bucking bronco. Being a housewife who enjoys reading as much as short story writing, I understand what it's like to just want to read a quick story to get the juices flowing and the beat in motion. Ladies! Grab your man and get wild for a few stolen minutes with the bedroom door is locked and enjoy your own private rodeo show. A mother needs those stolen moments with her man the most. Yeehaw!

Made in the USA
Middletown, DE
09 February 2024